Frankenstein

Mary Shelley

About this Book

For the Student

Listen to the story and do some activities on your Audio CD

Talk about the story

tune• When you see the orange dot you can check the word in the glossary

P Prepare for Cambridge English: Preliminary (PET) for Schools

For the Teacher

HELBLING e-ZONE THE EDUCATIONAL PLATFORM A state-of-the-art interactive learning environment with 1000s of free online self-correcting activities for your chosen readers.

Go to our Readers Resource site for information on using readers and downloadable Resource Sheets, photocopiable Worksheets and Answer Keys. Plus free sample tracks from the story.

www.helblingreaders.com

For lots of great ideas on using Graded Readers consult Reading Matters, the Teacher's Guide to using Helbling Readers.

Level 5 Structures

Modal verb *would*	Non-defining relative clauses
I'd love to...	Present perfect continuous
Future continuous	*Used to / would*
Future perfect	*Used to / used to doing*
Reported speech / verbs / questions	Second conditional
Past perfect	Expressing wishes and regrets
Defining relative clauses	

Structures from lower levels are also included

CONTENTS

HELBLING DIGITAL

e·ZONE
THE EDUCATIONAL PLATFORM

HELBLING e-zone is an inspiring new state-of-the-art, easy-to-use interactive learning environment.

The online self-correcting activities include:

- reading comprehension;
- listening comprehension;
- vocabulary;
- grammar;
- exam preparation.

TEACHERS register free of charge to set up classes and assign individual and class homework sets. Results are provided automatically once the deadline has been reached and detailed reports on performance are available at a click.

STUDENTS test their language skills in a stimulating interactive environment. All activities can be attempted as many times as necessary and full results and feedback are given as soon as the deadline has been reached. Single student access is also available.

FREE INTERACTIVE ONLINE TEACHING AND LEARNING MATERIALS

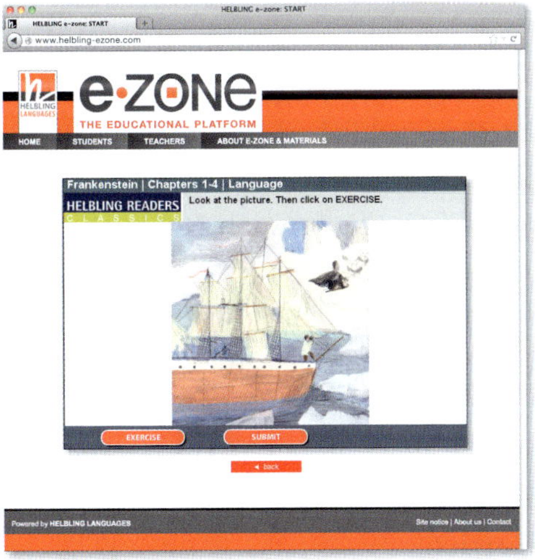

1000s of free online interactive activities now available for HELBLING READERS and your other favourite Helbling Languages publications.

www. helbling-ezone.com
ONLINE ACTIVITIES

blog.helblingreaders.com

NEW

Love reading and readers and can't wait to get your class interested? Have a class library and reading programme but not sure how to take it a step further? The Helbling Readers BLOG is the place for you.

The **Helbling Readers BLOG** will provide you with ideas on setting up and running a Book Club and tips on reading lessons **every week**.

- Book Club
- Worksheets
- Lesson Plans

Subscribe to our **BLOG** and you will never miss out on our updates.

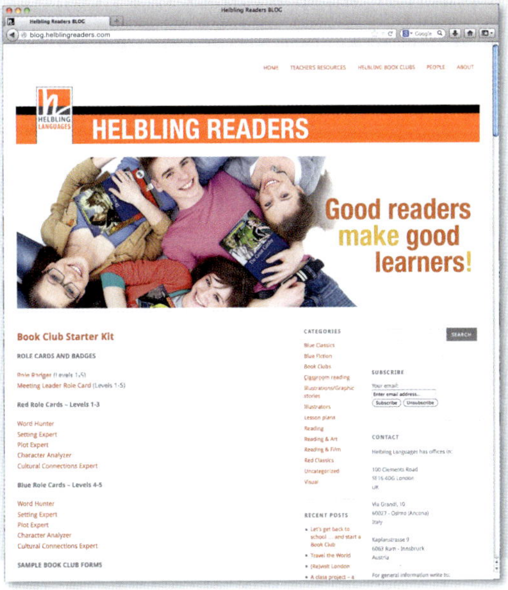

About the Author

Mary Wollstonecraft Shelley was born Mary Godwin in 1797. She was an English writer and wrote novels, short stories, plays and travel books. *Frankenstein*, published anonymously in 1818 when she was 20, is her best-known work. She was married to the English Romantic• poet Percy Bysshe Shelley.

Mary's mother died when Mary was only eleven days old. Her father married his neighbour, Mary Jane Clairmont, four years later. In 1814, Mary Godwin fell in love with Shelley, who was married. Together with Mary's stepsister, Claire Clairmont, they left for France and travelled around Europe. They married in 1816 after the suicide• of Shelley's first wife, Harriet.

In 1816, Mary and Percy spent their summer holiday with Lord Byron and other friends near Geneva, Switzerland. This was where Mary began writing *Frankenstein*, after the friends had a competition for the best horror story. The Shelleys left Britain in 1818 for Italy. They had two children but both of them died. Finally Mary had a son, Percy. But in 1822, her husband died. His boat sank during a storm and he drowned•. A year later, Mary returned to England. She looked after her son and earned money as a writer. She was ill for the last ten years of her life. She finally died of a brain tumour• at the age of 53.
Until the 1970s, Mary Shelley was known mainly for *Frankenstein*. But recently her other historical novels *Valperga* (1823) and travel books *Rambles• in Germany and Italy* (1844) were discovered.

Glossary

- **brain tumour:** cancer of the brain
- **drowned:** died in water
- **rambles:** walks
- **Romantic:** a group of English poets of the 18th century
- **suicide:** killing oneself

About the Book

Frankenstein is a novel about a young science student who creates a creature as a scientific experiment. It is a great horror story but also discusses ideas about philosophy and questions man's right to 'play God'. It is a very early example of science fiction.

During the summer of 1816, Mary Shelley travelled to Geneva with her husband Percy Shelley, Lord Byron, and others. The weather was too bad for outdoor activities, so the friends spent time inside. They read ghost stories and then had a competition to write the best horror story. Mary dreamt about a scientist who created life but was horrified by the 'thing' he had made; her dream became the story of *Frankenstein*.

As well as being a warning about the dangers of obsession•, the novel also talks about the problem of being lonely. The monster only becomes violent because he is rejected• for his appearance, not because he is naturally evil•. He shows himself to have a good character several times in his story.

When the book came out one critic said it was 'horrible and disgusting'. Others were shocked that a woman had written it. But *Frankenstein* was extremely popular. It became widely known when it was made into a stage play in 1823. It has inspired many films, TV adaptations and plays since then.

• **evil:** opposite of good; bad
• **obsession:** thinking of only one thing
• **rejected:** not accepted

Before Reading

1 What do you know about the novel *Frankenstein*? Tick (✓) true (T) or false (F).

	T	F
a) The novel is a horror story.	☐	☐
b) Frankenstein is the name of the monster.	☐	☐
c) The author was a woman.	☐	☐
d) The story has a happy ending.	☐	☐
e) Part of the story takes place at the North Pole.	☐	☐

2 Match the sentences to the characters. Then listen and check.

a) A science student who creates a monster as an experiment.
b) An explorer who travels to the North Pole on a ship.
c) A girl who grows up with Victor Frankenstein's family.
d) A boy who has blond hair and blue eyes.
e) A very large man, who has superhuman powers.
f) Victor Frankenstein's good friend, who loves anything medieval, especially King Arthur.

Victor Frankenstein

The monster

Elizabeth

Henry Clerval

Robert Walton

William Frankenstein

3 Look at the picture of Frankenstein and his monster. Read the passage then answer the questions.

Finally, one dark November night I completed my work. I collected my instruments and gave life to the being that lay at my feet. By the light of the candle, I saw the eyes of the creature open; it breathed hard, then made quick movements of its legs and arms.

How can I describe my emotions when I saw this disaster that with such endless work and care I had tried to create? I had selected his features as beautiful. Beautiful? Great God! His yellow skin only just covered the muscles and veins beneath; he had shiny black hair; his teeth were pearly white. But these good features only made a more unpleasant contrast with his watery eyes, lined face and straight black lips.

a) When did Frankenstein complete his work?

b) What colour was the creature's skin?

c) Did Frankenstein think the monster was beautiful?

d) What were the monster's good features?

e) What were his bad features?

f) Find the words in the text that mean the following.
1 tools .... 2 wrinkled ....
3 feelings .... 4 chosen ....

g) Which of these words does Frankenstein NOT use to describe his creation here? Tick (✓).

☐ being ☐ creature ☐ disaster ☐ monster

Before Reading

1 **Look at the names of some of the places mentioned in the story. Discuss with a partner what you know about them. Then look at a world map to see where they are.**

North Pole Russia Geneva Ingolstadt
London Perth (Scotland) Orkneys Naples Ireland

2 **Frankenstein gets his parts for the monster from three places. Match the places below with their definitions.**

a) ☐ cemetery
b) ☐ slaughterhouse
c) ☐ dissecting room

1 a room where dead bodies are cut up for scientific study
2 a place where dead people are buried
3 a place where animals are killed

3 **Complete the sentences with the correct word from Exercise 2.**

a) Frankenstein found body parts for the monster in the .... at his university.

b) He found animal body parts for the monster at the ....

c) After he died, Frankenstein's brother was buried in the .... in Geneva.

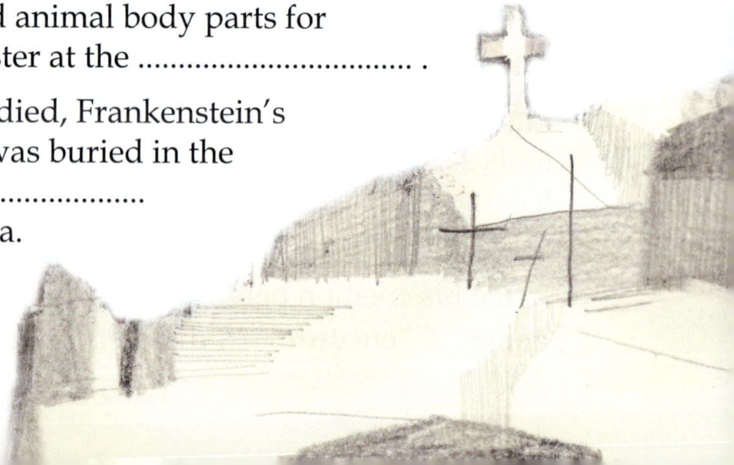

4 Write the correct words at the end of each sentence, using the words in the box below.

tombs	philosophy	professors	veins	physiology
anatomy	chemistry	decay	muscles	students

a) Two kinds of people you would find at a university.

....

b) Four names of subjects studied at university.

....

c) Two words for parts of the body.

....

d) One word for small buildings where the dead are buried.

....

e) One word that means breaking down; becoming only bones.

....

P 5 Choose the best word (1, 2 or 3) to complete the sentences.

a) Mr Waldman, the chemistry professor, said that I should study natural .... and mathematics.
1 muscles 2 philosophy 3 tombs

b) After that, natural philosophy and .... were my only occupation.
1 muscles 2 professors 3 chemistry

c) My main interest was the living body. I studied physiology and ....
1 decay 2 tombs 3 anatomy

d) I spent days and nights in ...., watching the decay of human bodies.
1 chemistry 2 physiology 3 tombs

e) The preparation of a body with all its muscles and ...., was extremely difficult.
1 students 2 philosophy 3 veins

Introduction

3 *In the year 17--•, an explorer, Robert Walton, travelled from England to Russia to find a way across the North Pole and into the Pacific Ocean. He wanted to be the first person to travel there by ship. He had been on many dangerous voyages•, and studied mathematics, science and medicine. Walton often wrote letters to his sister in England to tell her about his travels. In one particular letter her told her a strange and terrifying story full of horror, agony• and anguish•.*

August 5th, 17--

My dear sister,

Something strange happened to us this week. Our ship was surrounded by ice and a thick fog. When the fog lifted, in the distance we saw a very large man on a sledge• pulled by dogs. He was travelling away from us. This was amazing because we were several hundred kilometres from land and other civilisation. The next morning the ice broke up, and while the sailors were getting ready to sail, they saw another man on a piece of ice! The man was frozen, thin and very tired. We immediately invited him to join our ship, but he said he first wanted to know where the ship was going. We told him we were going to the North Pole and he agreed to join us.

He said he was following someone who had run away from him. I told him about the very large man we had seen the day before. He became excited and asked me lots of questions. Then he told me his story, as a warning• to me and to all men. So now, dear sister, I will tell you the story that the man told me.

Glossary

- **17--:** exact date not known
- **agony:** pain
- **anguish:** worry and sadness
- **sledge:** vehicle for travelling over snow
- **voyages:** long sea journeys
- **warning:** indication of possible danger

Chapter 1

4 My name is Victor Frankenstein and I am from Geneva. My father was a rich businessman and well-known in Switzerland. He married a poor woman, much younger than him. They travelled around Europe a lot and I was born in Naples.

My mother often visited poor people to help them. Once, near Lake Como, she visited a family with five hungry children. One little girl was slim and fair, different from the others. When my mother asked about her, the woman of the house said she was an orphan• and that her parents had been rich. My parents agreed to take her and bring her up with their own family.

The girl's name was Elizabeth, and she became my best friend. She was interested in poetry and nature, while I studied the physical secrets of the world and how things worked. On the birth of my youngest brother, when I was seven, my parents stopped travelling and returned to Geneva, living in our town house and a country house by the lake.

My other close friend was Henry Clerval, the son of a merchant•. Henry loved anything medieval•, especially King Arthur and his knights. He often tried to make us act plays and become characters from the medieval world of chivalry•. Henry was interested in morals• and heroes and he wanted to become one when he grew up. We had a happy childhood. Elizabeth was good and kind and she watched over us with her soft smile and beautiful eyes.

Glossary

- **chivalry:** the good behaviour of knights
- **medieval:** of the Middle Ages
- **merchant:** businessman who sells goods in large quantities
- **morals**: good behaviour
- **orphan:** child with no living parents

Despite my happy and carefree• childhood I was always eager• to learn about other things. It was the secrets of heaven and earth that I wanted to learn about. When I was thirteen I found a volume of the works of Cornelius Agrippa. This opened up a whole new world for me and I was very happy.

AGRIPPA

Use the Internet to find out more about Cornelius Agrippa. Discuss your findings in small groups.

My father told me not to waste my time reading such books and did not explain anything to me. So I read on alone, following what I read from a child's point of view, not properly understanding but still curious to learn.

This continued until a few years later when I saw the effects of a thunderstorm. A flash of lightning had completely destroyed a tree and a learned• guest staying with our family told us all about a theory• he had formed on the subject of electricity and galvanism•. These subjects were new and interesting for me and, pushing my years of studying Agrippa to one side, I immediately threw myself into the study of mathematics and science.

This was perhaps the last time that my 'guardian angel' tried to protect me from the storm that even then was waiting to fall on me.

Glossary

- **carefree:** without worries
- **galvanism:** movement made by an electric current
- **learned:** clever; knowing lots
- **theory:** idea
- **was eager:** wanted

Chapter 2

5 At seventeen, the first misfortune• of my life happened. Elizabeth caught scarlet fever•, and my mother looked after her. Soon, Elizabeth was cured, but my mother caught a terrible form of the illness and died. On her deathbed, she said that she hoped Elizabeth and I would marry.

I then left Geneva for the University of Ingolstadt. I was alone for the first time. My life had been extremely limited, and as I travelled, I thought with pleasure about the new knowledge that was waiting for me.

I immediately went to visit the main professors. Chance - or rather the Angel of Destruction, who was now in charge of• my life - led me first to Mr Krempe, professor of natural philosophy•. He was horrified that I had studied old writers like Cornelius Agrippa. He said I had completely wasted my time, then he wrote down a list of recent books that I should buy and read. However, I decided not to go to his lectures• because Mr Krempe was an ugly, short, fat man with an unpleasant• voice.

TEACHERS

What are your teachers like?

Tell a friend who is your worst teacher and why.

Do you think it is important for your teacher to be nice or good at teaching?

Discuss in small groups.

- **in charge of:** controlled
- **lectures:** lessons at university
- **misfortune:** bad luck
- **natural philosophy:** the study of nature; an early form of natural science
- **scarlet fever:** an infectious disease
- **unpleasant:** not nice

I then went to see Mr Waldman, the chemistry professor. He was very different: about 50 years old, with a kind expression and a very sweet voice. His first lecture began with a history of chemistry, and recent developments. He then described the current state of the sciences, and explained many basic terms•. He also did a few experiments, and then said: 'The ancient teachers of science promised impossibilities and performed nothing. The modern masters promise very little, but they have indeed performed miracles. They have got new and almost unlimited powers•.'

As he said this, I felt truly alive. His words touched the centre of my being, and soon my mind was filled with one thought: so much has been done, but I, Frankenstein, will do more. I will find new ways, explore unknown powers and open the world to the deepest mysteries of creation.

I returned to my old studies and devoted myself to• a science for which I believed I had a natural talent. When I visited Mr Waldman and told him about my earlier studies, he said that I should also study natural philosophy and mathematics, as every chemist needed that knowledge. He also gave me a list of books to buy. This was a memorable day which decided my future destiny•.

Glossary

- **destiny:** events happening in my life
- **devoted myself to:** followed exclusively
- **powers:** abilities to do things
- **terms:** words; phrases

Chapter 3

6 After that, natural philosophy and chemistry were my only occupation. I read the books and attended the lectures. My progress was quick, surprising the other students and my professors. After two years of continual study and experiment, I made improvements in some chemical instruments which brought me great respect at the university. I had by then reached a point where the University of Ingolstadt could no longer help my development. I was planning to return to Geneva when something happened which made me stay longer.

My main interest was the living body. Where did life come from? It was a big mystery. I studied physiology and anatomy. I spent days and nights in tombs• watching the decay• of human bodies. And then after days and nights of work, I discovered the cause of life, and, more importantly, I became able to create movement in lifeless matter•.

I thought about how to use this amazing power. For, although I could give life, the preparation of a body to receive it, with all its muscles• and veins•, was extremely difficult. Eventually•, I decided to make my own creation. It would be two and a half metres tall and also broad, because the small size of much of the body created difficulties. After some months of collecting and arranging my materials, I began.

Glossary

- **decay:** (here) breaking down; becoming only bones
- **eventually:** finally
- **matter:** substances; things
- **muscles:** tissues in body necessary for movement
- **tombs:** small buildings where the dead are buried
- **veins:** tubes in body that move blood to the heart

I was filled with enthusiasm• and energy. I could break through the knowledge of life and death and bring light into our dark world. I wanted to produce a new species• that would bless• me as its creator. I hoped that in time I would be able to bring back life after death. I worked day and night, I grew thin and pale. I collected bones from the cemetery•, and the dissecting room• and slaughterhouse• provided other parts I needed. I worked in a separate room at the top of the house. At times I hated what I was doing, but a wild passion made me continue.

In all this time I had no contact with my family. I never noticed the passing seasons. I kept away from fellow students. I slept badly and was often nervous and afraid, but still my purpose• burned in my mind like a bright light leading me on.

PURPOSE

Have you ever had a purpose or project that
kept you awake until you finished it?
Something like a book you were reading, a project
for school, a video you were making
or a game you were playing?
How did it make you feel?
Tell a friend.

- **bless:** love and bring luck to
- **cemetery:** place were the dead are buried
- **dissecting room:** place where dead bodies are cut up for scientific study
- **enthusiasm:** great interest
- **purpose:** reason for doing something
- **slaughterhouse:** place where animals are killed for food
- **species:** group of animals or plants able to recreate

Chapter 4

7 Finally, one dark November night, I completed my work. I collected my instruments and gave life to the being• that lay at my feet. By the light of the candle, I saw the eyes of the creature open; it breathed hard, then made quick movements of its legs and arms.

How can I describe my emotions• when I saw this disaster• that with such endless• work and care I had tried to create? I had selected his features as beautiful. Beautiful?! Great God!! His yellow skin only just covered the muscles and veins beneath; he had shiny black hair; his teeth were pearly white. But these good features• only made a more unpleasant contrast with his watery eyes, his lined face and straight black lips.

I had worked hard for nearly two years but now that I had finished, the beauty of the dream had disappeared. Horror and disgust filled my heart. I rushed• out of the room and lay on my bed and tried to forget about my creation. But when I awoke in the night, by the yellow light of the moon, I saw the miserable monster I had created. He stood by my bed and looked at me. His mouth opened and he made a sound I could not understand, and grinned•. I rushed past him and spent the rest of the night walking up and down nervously outside.

Glossary

- **being:** thing; creature
- **disaster:** terrible event
- **emotions:** feelings
- **endless:** without end; very long
- **features:** elements; aspects
- **grinned:** smiled
- **rushed:** went quickly

At six o'clock I went out into the wet, grey streets, terrified of meeting the creature at every corner. I hurried on, soaked• by the pouring rain. I came to an inn• where coaches• from other places stopped. To my surprise a Swiss coach stopped, and Henry Clerval got out.

'My dear Frankenstein!' he said. 'I'm so glad you were here exactly when I arrived!'

I was delighted to see Clerval, my dear childhood friend. He brought back memories of my father, Elizabeth and all those scenes of home that were important to me. In a moment I forgot my horror and misery•. For the first time in many months, I felt calm and happy. We walked to my apartment, while Henry talked about our friends and families.

'But, my dear Frankenstein,' he continued, 'how thin and pale you are, as if you had been up for several nights.'

'You are right,' I replied. 'Recently I have been so busy with one project that I have not allowed myself to rest, but it is finished now, and finally I am free.'

I shook as we walked. I thought the creature might still be in my apartment, and I feared that Henry would see him. So I was delighted to find the apartment empty. We had breakfast, but I could not sit still. I jumped up, clapped my hands and laughed aloud.

'Victor!' Henry cried, 'Don't laugh like that! How ill you are! What is the matter?'

'Don't ask me,' I cried, putting my hands over my eyes. 'Save me, save me!'

Glossary

- **coaches:** vehicles moved by horses
- **inn:** hotel; pub
- **misery:** great sadness
- **soaked:** made completely wet

This was the start of a nervous fever which kept me in my room for several months. Henry was my only nurse. During my illness, the monster was always before my eyes, and I talked madly about him. Slowly I recovered and by the following spring, I felt much better.

'Dearest Clerval!' I said one morning. 'How very good you are to me. Instead of studying, you have spent the whole winter in my sick room. How can I repay • you?'

'Get well as fast as you can,' he replied. 'And write a letter to your father and Elizabeth. They would be happy to receive a letter in your own handwriting.'

'Of course I will,' I said.

'Well since you feel so happy,' he answered, 'perhaps you would like to see this letter from Elizabeth? It has been here for some days.'

The letter from Elizabeth said she was delighted to hear of my recovery •, and hoped I would write soon. She told me that my father was very well and that my brother Ernest was now sixteen and wanted to become a soldier. My youngest brother William was now tall and attractive, with blue eyes and curly hair. She ended by saying how grateful they were that Henry had looked after me so well.

- **recovery:** getting better
- **repay:** give you something back in return

Later, I introduced Henry to my university professors. I was embarrassed when both Mr Waldman and Mr Krempe talked highly of my work. But wanting to forget everything that had brought me to my nervous state and the creation of that monster, I abandoned my previous studies. Instead I chose to follow Henry and his studies of Oriental languages.

I had planned to return to Geneva in the autumn, but I didn't want to leave Clerval on his own in a strange place. And then the winter snows came and the roads were blocked. In May of the following year Henry and I went on a walking tour of the Ingolstadt region, spending two weeks exploring the area. It was a very happy time, with much good conversation, too, and I returned to Ingolstadt healthy and full of energy.

Chapter 5

When I returned home I found the following letter from my father:

My dear Victor,

You have probably been waiting for a letter from me to plan the date of your return. However, I'm afraid your return will not be a happy one. William is dead! Victor, he is murdered!

Last Thursday Elizabeth, your two brothers and I went for a walk at Plainpalais•. We went further than usual, but as we returned Elizabeth and I could not find Ernest and William. They were playing hide and seek•. Then Ernest returned saying he could not find William. We searched until night fell, then went home, thinking that perhaps he was there. He was not. We returned, with torches, to keep searching. At about five in the morning, I discovered my lovely son, with the signs of the murderer's hands on his neck.

Elizabeth blamed herself•, because she had let William wear a valuable necklace with a miniature painting of his mother on it... and this was missing•. It was certainly what the murderer wanted.

Come home now and help us to get over• our deep feelings of sadness and loss•.

Your affectionate father,
Alphonse Frankenstein

Tears poured from my eyes. I threw the letter down and indicated that Clerval should read it. When he had finished, he said: 'There is nothing I can say to help, my friend. This loss is a disaster you cannot repair. What are you going to do?'

'I'll go to Geneva straight away.'

Glossary

- **blamed herself:** thought it was her fault; that she caused it to happen
- **get over:** recover from; forget
- **hide and seek:** game where children hide and another child tries find them
- **loss:** having lost something
- **missing:** not there
- **Plainpalais:** an area of Geneva

On my journey I was filled with mixed feelings: sadness at my little brother's death, and joy at seeing my father, Elizabeth and Ernest after nearly six years. When I finally saw Lake Geneva and the mountains around it I cried with happiness. I decided to first visit Plainpalais where William had died. I went by boat across the lake and as I landed•, a spectacular thunderstorm started, growing stronger, with pouring rain and flashes of lightning illuminating the lake. It raised my spirits, and I shouted: 'William, dear Angel! This is your funeral• and your funeral song.'

Suddenly, a flash of lightning illuminated a figure coming out from behind some trees. I could not be wrong. It was the horrible monster to which I had given life! How had he come here? Had he murdered my brother? I became sure that it was true. He continued past me, and in the next flash of lightning I saw him easily climbing the cliffs of a nearby mountain.

I didn't move. The rain continued. It was now two years since he had received life. Had I created a creature that enjoyed killing and making others unhappy? I stayed there the whole night, wet and in a state of great worry. Was the creature going to destroy everything that was important to me?

At five o'clock I arrived at my father's house, so I went into the library to rest. Some time later, my brother Ernest came in.

'Welcome, my dearest Victor,' he said. 'But I wish you had come three months ago and found us all happy. I hope you will comfort• our father, and stop Elizabeth blaming herself for William's death.'

Glossary

- **comfort:** make someone feel better
- **funeral:** ceremony in which a dead person is buried
- **landed:** arrived on land

Tears poured from our eyes, as Ernest explained more about Elizabeth: 'She accuses herself of having caused our brother's death, but since they have found the murderer...'

'Found the murderer!' I shouted. 'Good God! How is that possible? Who could follow him? I saw him, too. He was free last night!'

'I do not know what you mean,' replied my brother, much surprised, 'because the discovery we have made completes our misery. Who would have thought that our servant• Justine Moritz, who was so kind and loving with all the family, could suddenly commit such an awful crime•?'

Ernest explained that on the morning after William's murder, Justine had felt ill and was in bed for several days. One of the servants had examined the clothes she had worn on the night of the murder, and found the necklace with our mother's picture in a pocket. The servants went to the magistrate• and Justine was arrested and charged•. She was extremely confused, which made everyone think she was responsible.

'You are all wrong,' I said. 'I know the murderer. Justine is innocent.'

When my father entered a few moments later, Ernest exclaimed: 'Father – Victor says that he knows who murdered poor William.'

'And so do we,' said my father. 'And I am sorry that one whom we loved and trusted should reward• us in this way.'

'Justine is innocent,' I said.

'If she is,' my father replied, 'we will find out today when she is tried• and set free•.'

Glossary

- **charged:** registered as the person who did a crime
- **crime:** illegal act
- **magistrate:** official person to judge crimes
- **reward:** (here) thank
- **servant:** person employed to work in someone's house
- **set free:** is able to go home
- **tried:** made to speak in front of officials to see if they did a crime

Chapter 6

9 Next morning we went to the law court•. Witnesses• reported several strange facts about Justine. She had been out the whole night of the murder. Then, towards morning, she was seen near where the body was found. She had been confused when asked what she was doing there. She had returned home about eight in the morning, saying she had looked for William. On seeing the body, she fell into violent hysterics• and stayed in bed for several days. The necklace with the picture was found in her pocket by a servant.

Justine then defended herself. She had passed the evening of the murder at an aunt's house, with Elizabeth's permission. When she returned she heard William was missing and so went out to look for him. She was out for many hours. As Geneva city gates were shut she could not return home, so she slept in the barn• of some people she knew, without disturbing• them. The next morning she looked for William again. If she went near where the body was found, it was by chance. If she had appeared confused, it was because of her lack of sleep, and her worry about William. She could say nothing about the necklace.

Then Elizabeth spoke: 'I have lived in the same house as Justine for seven years. She looked after Madame Frankenstein in her final illness with great affection and care. She was strongly attached to William. As for the necklace – the main proof• – I would happily give it to her. I believe Justine is absolutely innocent.'

- **barn:** large farm building
- **disturbing:** (here) waking
- **hysterics:** showing great emotion and sadness
- **law court:** place to judge legal cases
- **proof:** object or fact that shows something is true
- **witnesses:** people who saw an event and talk about it; (here) in a law court

However, the crowd wanted someone to be responsible for this horrible murder, and the magistrate condemned• poor Justine. Next morning, they told me that she had confessed. Later, we visited Justine in prison. She said she had only confessed so that she could receive absolution• and that she was ready to die.

I now felt that I was the true murderer.

After Justine's death, I looked around our once-happy family. Everyone was destroyed and in deepest misery because of the deaths of William and Justine, and it was all the work of my hands. I was unable to sleep. I had done terrible things. I had begun with good intentions - to be useful to my fellow beings. But I had destroyed everything. Instead of looking back happily on my achievements and looking forward with hope to new discoveries, I felt only regret•, horror, despair• and guilt•.

REGRET

Do you think Victor Frankenstein
is right to feel this way?
Why?
Discuss in small groups.

Glossary

- **condemned:** gave a punishment to
- **despair:** being without hope
- **guilt:** feeling of having done something wrong
- **receive absolution:** be clear of sin
- **regret:** sad about something you did or didn't do

Chapter 7

We then moved to our house beside the lake. At night I often took the boat and passed many hours on the water. I felt like throwing myself into the silent lake so that the water would close over my miseries forever. But I stopped myself by thinking of Elizabeth, whom I loved so sweetly, and who suffered so much.

Every day I feared the monster would do some new evil act. I had a feeling that he had not finished. I wished I could kill the creature which I had so thoughtlessly• created. My desire for revenge• and my hate of him filled my whole body and mind. I wanted to take revenge for the deaths of William and Justine.

Sometimes, in such states of passion, I needed physical exercise and a change of place. So, in mid-August, I went walking in the Alpine valleys near Chamonix. The weather was fine, and the scenery of the Alps themselves was spectacular. I felt pleasure amongst the wonders of nature, but then my horror and despair would return. When I finally got to Chamonix, both my mind and my body were exhausted, and I slept deeply that night.

The following morning, it was pouring with rain. The mountains were covered in thick cloud. But I set out to climb Montanvert•. It was difficult on the narrow path, but by midday I was at the top. The wind blew the cloud away, and I went down onto the glacier• and crossed it.

- **glacier:** slowly moving mass of ice
- **Montanvert:** area in the Alps
- **revenge:** doing something bad in return for something bad someone did to you
- **thoughtlessly:** without thinking

I could now see Mont Blanc. It was a spectacular view – the river of ice surrounded by icy peaks•.

As I looked, I suddenly saw a large man coming towards me at superhuman speed. I realized that it was the monster I had created. I was filled with anger and horror, and decided to fight him to the death.

'Devil!' I shouted. 'Do you dare• to come near me? Aren't you afraid that I will take my revenge?'

'I expected this,' he said. 'People hate all ugly things, and I am uglier than them all. But you, my creator, you want to kill me? How dare you play with life like this? Do your duty• towards me, and I will do my duty towards you and all mankind•. If you agree, I will leave you and them in peace. If not, then I will kill and destroy all your remaining friends.'

'Monster! Devil!' I screamed. 'You blame me for your creation. Well, come here and let me end the life which I so thoughtlessly gave you!'

I jumped at him, but he easily moved out of the way, and said: 'Please listen to me. I have suffered enough. I am your creature, and I will be gentle with you if you will give me what you owe• me. Oh, Frankenstein, don't be kind to everyone else and unkind to me alone. I see happiness everywhere which I cannot have. I was kind and good; misery made me into a monster. Make me happy and I'll be good.'

Glossary

- **dare:** have the courage
- **duty:** what is right
- **mankind:** people in the world
- **owe:** must pay or give
- **peaks:** tops of mountains

'Go away!' I shouted. 'I will not listen to you. We are enemies. Go away, or let us fight until one of us dies.'

'I really was good, but I am alone,' he said. 'If you hate me then what can I expect from others? The world hates me, so why should I not hate everyone? But you can change this. Come to the barn where I have made my shelter• and listen to my story before you judge me finally. It is in your power to save me. You can decide whether I lead a good life, or whether I become a devil for your fellow beings and the cause of your own destruction. Listen to me, Frankenstein!'

Partly because I was curious and partly because I felt sorry for the monster, I followed him across the ice. Soon we were seated by the fire near his shelter and he began his tale.

LISTEN

Do you think it is important to listen to a person's story before judging them?
Why?
Can you think of a time when you judged someone and then found out later that their story was completely different? How did you feel when you found out the real story?
Tell a friend.

Glossary

• **shelter:** safe place to stay

Chapter 8

11 And so the monster began:

'At first I was confused by everything. I lived in the woods near Ingolstadt. Gradually, I learned to recognise the birds, insects, plants and trees. I once found a fire, left by others, and so I learnt how to keep myself warm at night. But I was very hungry, and I looked for food. I found a small barn where an old man was making breakfast. On seeing me, he screamed and ran away as fast as he could. I ate his breakfast, then I lay down and slept.

'I awoke at noon and walked on. At sunset I reached a village. It seemed wonderful – the barns, cottages and bigger houses, many with milk and cheese in the windows. I entered one of the better houses, but the children screamed and one of the women fainted •. The whole village came: some ran away, and some attacked me. I left.

'Eventually, I found a small building next to an isolated cottage •. It was simple but dry. I was also able to look out through gaps • in the walls, and see into the cottage through a gap in one of them. A little later, a young woman arrived. A young man met her and they went into the cottage. Inside the room I saw an old man who looked very unhappy. The girl was doing various jobs. Then she gave the old man a guitar and he began to play, while she sang. It was beautiful. The young man returned later with wood for the fire, a loaf and cheese. The girl cooked some plants from the garden, and they all ate. Then night fell and the family went to sleep.

- **fainted:** lost consciousness
- **gaps:** holes
- **isolated cottage:** cottage on its own; with no other cottages nearby

'I thought about what I had seen and the people's gentle manners•. I wanted to join them, but I decided to stay there quietly, to observe and understand them. I watched them working. I also noticed that the young man and woman treated the old man with love and respect, but sometimes they went off together and cried. I couldn't understand why.

'Later I understood that they were very poor and hungry. Previously I had sometimes stolen their food, but after that I lived on what I could find from the woods. I also helped them. I cut wood for them at night, as the young man spent much of the day looking for wood for the fire. At first they were very surprised, but then they spent the days repairing the cottage and working in the garden. Through watching and listening to them I learnt a lot of basic words, and also the names of the three: *father; brother* or *son* or *Felix; sister* or *Agatha*. As the winter progressed, I learnt more of their words. The father was blind•, so the son sometimes read to him. I wanted to meet these sweet, kind people, but I realised that I needed to be able to use their language well. I admired their beauty and I knew that I was monstrous• because I had seen myself reflected• in a pool of water.

'My daily life was almost always the same. I watched the people in the morning, slept in the middle of the day, watched them again in the afternoon and evening, and then if it was a clear night, I went out into the woods to collect my own food, and to cut wood for them. As spring arrived I had happy feelings in my heart.

Glossary

- **blind:** not able to see
- **manners:** ways
- **monstrous:** like a monster
- **reflected:** when an image is shown (like in a mirror)

'One day, a lady arrived at the cottage. When Felix saw her, his sadness disappeared and a great change began in their lives. She met his sister and father, but she could not speak their language, nor they hers. They started teaching her their language and so I followed them very carefully. The lady was called Safie, and she and I improved our language quickly. I also learned to read as she did, and learnt about history and society through the book that Felix used to teach her.

'However, I also realised that I was lower than the lowest human. There was no one like me. Was I a monster that all men ran from and nobody wanted? The gentle words of Agatha and Safie were not for me, nor the conversation of the old man and Felix. They talked of families, friends and children, but where were mine? My past life was completely empty. I had always been the same height and size, and I had never seen another being like me. What was I?'

PAST

Can you imagine not having a past? How would you feel?
Tell a friend about your past.

Chapter 9

12 The monster continued:

'After a time, I realised that although there were similarities between me and human beings, there was one big difference: I was dependent on nobody and had no relatives. Nobody would miss me when I was gone. I was ugly to look at and very big. What did this mean? Who was I? What was I? Where did I come from?

But as I could now read, I looked at some papers of yours which I had kept. They were the four months of your journal before my creation. You described everything in detail. It showed your horror at what you were doing. I felt sicker and sicker as I read it. I wondered why you had created a monster so horrible that even you turned away in disgust. But my neighbours were so good that I wanted to be their friend, to take part in their happiness. I had seen that they never turned away poor people who stopped at their door, and felt they would not turn me away in horror.

'I thought of how I could introduce myself to them. I decided it would be best to enter the cottage when the blind old man was alone. I knew that my hideous• appearance was the main cause of people's horror. I felt that if I could get the old man on my side, the younger neighbours might tolerate• me. Then one sunny winter's afternoon Safie, Agatha and Felix went for a long country walk, and I took my chance. I knocked at the cottage door.

"Who is there?" asked the old man. "Come in."

'I entered. "Excuse me," I said, "I am a traveller in need of rest. Could I sit by your fire for a few minutes?"

"Come in," said the old man, "I am blind and my children are away from home, so I cannot find food for you. Are you French?"

"No," I replied, "but I was educated by a French family. I now want to get protection from some friends whom I love, and whom I hope will help me. But they have never seen me, and I am afraid, because if I cannot make friends with them, I will be alone in the world forever."

"That is very sad," he answered. "If you tell me your story perhaps I can help."

"Thank you," I said happily. "I accept your generous offer. I hope that with your help they will not send me away."

"May I know the names of these friends and where they live?" he asked.

'I took his hand and said: "You and your family are these friends. Do not leave me to suffer alone."

"Great God!" exclaimed the old man. "Who are you?"

'At that moment, the cottage door opened and Felix, Safie and Agatha entered. It is impossible to describe their horror on seeing me. Agatha fainted, Safie rushed out of the cottage, and Felix jumped forward, and pulled his father from me, pushing me to the ground and hitting me violently with a stick. My heart sank and I felt sick. I was filled with pain and worry. I left the cottage, and managed to get back into my home without being seen.

'O my damned creator! I was in such misery. When night came I went out into the woods, wandering• and howling•. There was nobody who would feel pity• for me or help me. I declared war against human beings, and more than all against my creator who had sent me out to face this terrible misery. After dark I went back to my home.

'Later, Felix appeared with another man, and I listened to their conversation.

"Do you realise that you will have to pay three months' rent• and lose the produce of your garden?" asked the man.

"We can never live in your cottage again after the events I described to you," said Felix. "Please, take back your cottage, and let me leave this place as quickly as possible."

'I never saw the family again. My only link to the world had gone. Feelings of revenge and hatred filled me. First, I destroyed everything in the garden. And then I set fire to the cottage.

MONSTER

Do you feel anger or pity for the monster?

- **hideous:** very ugly
- **howling:** making a sound like a dog
- **pity:** sadness
- **rent:** money paid for living in someone's house
- **tolerate:** allow to exist; accept
- **wandering:** walking around

'I decided to look for you next. You were the only one who I could ask for pity. I knew from your journal that you lived in Geneva. But how could I find the way? The sun was my only guide as I could not ask directions from any humans. My travels were long and I suffered greatly. It was late autumn when I started out, travelling only at night to avoid meeting anyone. It rained and snowed, great rivers became frozen, and the earth was cold and bare•. By early spring I reached Switzerland.

'One day, I was travelling through a forest. I did not hide and rest as usual, because it was so beautiful and I felt happy. I came to a deep, fast river when I heard voices, so I ran behind a tree. A little girl ran along laughing, but slipped• and fell into the river. I climbed down with great difficulty to save her. She was unconscious•, and I was trying to help her when the man who had been with her appeared. He rushed up and grabbed• the girl from me and ran off. I followed him, without knowing why, but he turned round and shot me.

'That was my reward! I had saved a human life, and now I was in pain. I decided to hate all humans, and to get revenge whenever I could. After several weeks in the wood, the wound• in my shoulder healed•.

Glossary

- **bare:** (here) without plants or vegetation
- **grabbed:** took quickly
- **healed:** got better
- **slipped:** lost her balance
- **unconscious:** not awake
- **wound:** cut; broken or open skin

'Then I travelled on towards Geneva, and hid in the fields nearby to decide what I should do to you.

'While I was there I was disturbed by the arrival of a beautiful child. I suddenly thought that he was innocent and would not be afraid of me. If I took him, I could educate him as my friend, and I would not be so lonely in the world. So I caught the boy as he passed. As soon as he saw me, he screamed and covered his eyes. I removed his hand from his face.

"I do not want to hurt you," I said. "Listen to me."

"Let me go!" he cried. "You're an ugly monster. You want to eat me. Let me go or I'll tell my father."

"You will never see your father again," I said. "You must come with me."

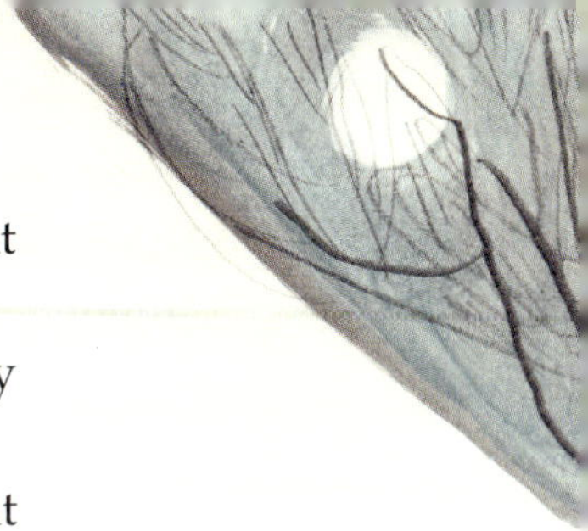

"Let me go!" he screamed. "My father is important – he's Mr Frankenstein. He will punish you!"

"Frankenstein!" I shouted. "You belong to my enemy! Then you'll be my first victim."

'I put my hands around his neck and in a moment he lay dead at my feet. As I looked at him I felt a kind of victory. I knew this death would bring despair to my enemy. Then I noticed he wore a necklace with a picture of a beautiful woman and I took it. I then looked for somewhere to hide, and entered a barn, but was surprised to find a young woman sleeping there. I looked at her and thought that no woman would ever love me. People can think that she is guilty for the murder of the boy, and she can be punished. So I dropped the necklace with the picture into her pocket.

'I stayed around that area, but eventually I wandered towards these mountains, where I have remained ever since. I am alone and miserable. Humans will have nothing to do with me, but a female as deformed• and horrible as myself would not refuse me. My companion must be of the same species as myself. You must create this being.'

He finished talking and stared at me. I only felt my anger at William's death.

'I refuse,' I said. 'Why should I create another creature for you both to do terrible things in the world? Go away!'

'You are wrong,' he replied. 'I am evil because I am miserable. Everyone hates me, so why should I pity them when they do not pity me? And if I cannot make people love me, then I will make them fear me. And my revenge will mainly be aimed at• you. Be careful, or I will destroy you.'

LOVE

Do you think love stops people from being bad?
Discuss in small groups.

Glossary

- **aimed at:** for
- **deformed:** not perfect or normal

I thought about what he had said, and realized that maybe if he was happy, he would not create problems for others again.

'If I agree,' I said, 'swear• that you will leave Europe forever as soon as I give you a female to go with you.'

'I swear,' he cried. 'If you agree you will never see me again. Now go and start your work. I'll watch your progress carefully, and when you are ready I will appear.'

He left and descended the mountain very quickly. I returned immediately to Geneva. I felt very unhappy about the whole situation before me, and could find almost no happiness when I saw my family again. To save them, I had to perform this awful task•.

TASK

What does Victor Frankenstein have to do?
Why is it so awful?

• **swear:** promise

• **task:** work to be done

Chapter 10

13 Many weeks passed, but I was unable to start my work. I was frightened that the monster would come, and I felt disgusted by what I had promised to do. One day my father said he wanted to talk to me.

'Victor, I have always looked forward to your marriage to Elizabeth. You have always been close to each other, so I wonder whether you now see her more as a sister and a friend?'

'Don't worry, father,' I replied. 'I hope that one day Elizabeth and I will get married.'

'This is wonderful news,' he replied. 'Are you interested in getting married soon?'

I thought of my promise to the creature. How could I get married and have a normal life before I had fulfilled• my terrible promise? I would need to hide somewhere secret to complete the horrible task. These feelings helped me answer my father's question. I said I needed to go to England first, without saying exactly why, for a period of up to a year. My father was happy to agree, hoping that the change would complete my physical and mental recovery.

In September, I left for England. I was worried the monster might hurt my family in my absence•, but believed that he would follow me to England, and so they would be safe. Henry Clerval came with me. We sailed down the Rhine to Rotterdam and got a ship to London.

Glossary

- **absence:** not being present
- **fulfilled:** done what he had promised

In London I met an important natural philosopher to find new information related to my unpleasant task. Henry was interested in going to India and started collecting information on how to organise it, while I gathered the materials I needed. We slowly made our way to Perth in Scotland, where we had been invited by a friend.

I was worried because I had still not started my work. I wondered what the creature might do. I left Clerval with our friend in Perth while I went to complete my task in a cottage on a remote island in the Orkneys further north. As time passed, I found it increasingly difficult to continue with my horrible work, and every moment I expected to look up and see the form of the monster before me.

Chapter 11

14 One night, I was thinking about what I was doing. I had no idea what this female creature might be like. My first creation had promised to leave Europe, but she might not agree. She might be even more evil than he was. And if they had children, then what race of creatures would I have started on earth?

I suddenly looked up and saw the monster outside, looking at me and grinning. He had followed me and was waiting for my work to end. But in his face I saw only evil. I thought how mad my promise to him had been. Trembling with fear, I tore the thing I had created to pieces before him. With a horrible howl of despair, he disappeared.

I went back to my own room. I heard footsteps and the sound of the door and I knew the monster had come.

'You destroyed your work,' he said. 'Do you dare to break your promise? I have been waiting and now you have destroyed my hopes.'

'Go away!' I shouted. 'I have broken my promise. I will never make another evil creature like you.'

'Remember that I have power,' he said. 'I can make your situation even worse. You are my creator, but I am your master. Obey!'

'You cannot make me do something wicked. I will not create an evil companion for you.' I shouted. 'Go away!'

'You will regret this,' cried the creature. 'Now, I am only interested in revenge. Remember this: I will be with you on your wedding night.'

'Monster!' I screamed. 'Before you think of killing me, make sure that you are safe yourself.'

He left quickly, and I later saw him sailing away in his boat. Then I started thinking of his threat: *I will be with you on your wedding night.* So I had until then to do something.

Two days later a letter from Clerval arrived, asking me to come back so we could return to London to complete his Indian business. I went to my laboratory and packed up all my instruments. I put all the horrible mess• of my work into a basket and filled it with stones. Later that night I sailed out to sea and dropped it over the side of my boat.

It was a peaceful, moonlit night, and I fell asleep on the boat. When I awoke the wind and waves were very strong. I could not control the boat, so I let the wind carry it. I looked at the clouds moving fast in the sky and then at the sea and I thought that I was going to die. Much, much later I was pleased to see land. It was calmer now, and I followed the coast until I came to a small harbour. People soon gathered• around as I tied up the boat.

Glossary

- **gathered:** came
- **mess:** dirty or untidy substance or state

'Excuse me,' I started, hearing them speak English. 'Can you tell me where I am, please?'

'You will know that soon enough,' said one man.

'Why do you answer me so rudely?' I asked.

'Because it is the custom• of the Irish to hate bad people,' he replied. 'You must follow me to Mr Kirwin to explain yourself.'

'Who is Mr Kirwin?' I asked. 'And why must I explain myself?'

'Mr Kirwin is the magistrate,' he said. 'And you are to explain the death of a man who was found murdered here last night.'

I was very surprised by this answer, and although exhausted and very hungry, I followed him, ready to prove my innocence.

IRELAND

Victor Frankenstein is now in Ireland.
Look at a map or on the Internet to follow his journey on the sea from the Orkney Islands to the northern coast of Ireland.

• **custom:** way; habit

Chapter 12

15 I was taken before the magistrate, who called for witnesses. A sailor explained how the night before they had returned to land some distance from the town, because of the strong winds and storm. They had found the still-warm body of a young man. Someone had strangled• him. On hearing this I shook, remembering my brother William.

Other witnesses saw a boat like mine with a single man in it near the place. I was then taken in to see the body. Imagine my feelings when I saw that it was Henry Clerval!

'Has my murderous behaviour killed you, too, Henry?' I shouted. 'I have already destroyed two. But you, Clerval, my friend, my helper...'

I fainted and was carried from the room. I lay in a bed for two months at the point of death, raving• about murdering William, Justine and now Clerval. Then one day I woke to find myself in prison. Kirwin visited me occasionally, to see how I was. One day he told me that my father was there.

My father gave me news that Elizabeth, Ernest and he were safe and well. After this first visit, my illness gradually left me, but my black mood• got worse. I had horrible images of the murdered Henry before me all the time. I hoped that I would be punished for the crime, and so end my own misery. I was in prison for three months before the court heard my case. The jury rejected it because there was proof that I was still on Orkney at the time when my friend's body was found, and soon I was set free from prison.

Glossary

- **cheer me up:** make me happier
- **mood:** state of mind
- **raving:** talking in a mad and semi-conscious way
- **strangled:** killed someone by tightening your hands around their neck

I wanted to return to Geneva quickly, so that I could look after the three people I loved so much. I wanted a chance to find where the monster was hiding, or if he dared to come to see me again, then to kill him. Of course I frequently remembered the creature's words: *I will be with you on your wedding night.* This is what would happen: he would kill me on that night. His power over me would end. I would finally be a free man. But this did not mean he would do nothing else before then. He had proved this by murdering Clerval.

Back in Geneva I was mostly in very low spirits and only Elizabeth was able to cheer me up•. We decided to get married in ten days' time. Arrangements for the wedding were made, and I prepared myself for the creature's attack. I carried pistols and a knife with me constantly. But as the days passed and the ceremony was closer, I began to hope that all might be well. After the ceremony, there was a large party at my father's house. We, however, went to Evian by boat, where we had planned to spend the night.

Chapter 13

We landed at eight o'clock, walked for a short time on the shore, enjoying the evening light, then returned to the inn where we were staying. A heavy rainstorm started and my fears returned. I held the pistol I was carrying and decided I would fight until either I or the creature were dead. I then thought how awful it would be for Elizabeth to see me fight to the death, so I asked her to go to bed. I continued walking along the corridors, looking for my enemy.

Suddenly I heard a dreadful scream. I rushed to our room and entered. Elizabeth was dead! The murderer had thrown her on the bed. I fainted and woke some time later. I then got up and held Elizabeth's cold body, and saw the mark of the monster's hands on her neck. Then as I looked out of the window, I saw him there, grinning and pointing at my dead wife. I rushed to the window and fired my pistol. He ran quickly to the lake and jumped in. People came running when they heard the gun shot. We followed but found nothing.

I returned immediately to Geneva fearing that my father and Ernest were in danger. When I arrived, they were still alive. My father, however, was shocked by the news about Elizabeth, and a few days later he died of sadness.

I told my story to a magistrate in Geneva, saying I knew who had destroyed my family, and asking him to find and capture• the murderer. He listened in disbelief• and horror. Finally he said he would happily look for the creature, but that as he seemed to have superhuman strength, he was not sure how capture would be possible. He said I should be prepared to be disappointed.

I told him that I wanted revenge, and if he could not help me, then I would do it myself.

I now hated Geneva. I left, taking money and jewels• which had belonged to my mother. I started these wanderings which will only stop when I die. I have travelled everywhere and I will not rest until my enemy is dead.

Before leaving I went to the cemetery where William, Elizabeth and my father were buried. I stood by their graves• and said out loud: 'I promise that I will live until I have taken revenge on this horrible monster, and made him feel the misery that I now feel.'

I heard a loud, evil laugh and then I heard the hated voice say: 'I am pleased, miserable man, that you have decided to live.'

In the moonlight I saw him running away faster than any human could.

Glossary

- **capture:** catch; find
- **disbelief:** not believing
- **graves:** places where dead people are buried
- **jewels:** precious stones

I followed him down the Rhône, over the Mediterranean and across Russia. I was often cold, hungry and exhausted. Sometimes the monster left signs for me – an arrow to show the direction he had taken, or a message: 'You live. My power is complete. Follow me.' 'I am going to the frozen north, where you will feel the misery of cold and frost, which I do not feel.' 'You will have many hard, miserable hours before we fight for our lives.'

I bought a sledge and dogs, and was able to catch up with him. When I got to the sea, I was only one day behind him. He had arrived the night before and had taken the villagers' sledge, dogs and all their winter food. He had set off across the frozen sea in a direction which did not lead to land. They believed he would die soon, either by the cold or because of the breaking ice.

I exchanged my sledge for one that would go better on the frozen sea, and bought a lot of food. Then I left the land. Sometimes mountains of ice blocked my way, and at other times I heard the ice melting, only for it to freeze again. Often I feared that I would never catch my enemy before I died, but then after struggling up some hill of ice I would see him in the distance, and I felt hopeful again. I got closer, and after two more days I was less than two kilometres behind him.

FOLLOW

Follow Frankenstein and the monster's journey on a map.

Glossary

- **arrow:** →
- **catch up with:** reach
- **melting:** slowly becoming liquid
- **struggling:** moving with difficulty

But just when I thought I would catch him, the ice started breaking up. Soon there was open sea between me and my enemy. I was in despair until I saw your ship. I directed my ice 'island' towards you. I was going to ask you for a boat in which to follow the monster. But you were going north, and you saved me from death. I was very pleased about this because my work was not yet completed. But if I die without having caught him, and you find him, Walton, promise me that you will kill him for me, to take revenge for the deaths of William, Justine, Clerval, Elizabeth and my father. And mine.

WALTON

Who is Walton? Go back to page 13 to check.

Conclusion

17 *Robert Walton finished writing Victor Frankenstein's story at the end of August 17--. He then went on to tell his sister what happened over the following few weeks.*

August 26th, 17--

My dear sister,

You have read this strange and terrifying story. Do you feel your blood run cold• with horror as mine does? Currently I am surrounded by ice which might break the ship at any moment. It is extremely cold, and several of my men have already died. Some sailors asked me to promise that when the ship was free, we go south. But Frankenstein asked them why they had come so far only to turn back; he praised• their courage, and said they would be heroes when they found the way through the ice to the Pacific Ocean, which was the aim of the expedition. He begged• them to continue. I asked them to consider what Frankenstein had said, but told them I would not continue further north if they decided against it.

September 9th, 17--

The ice began to move. By this time Frankenstein was very weak.

Glossary

- **begged:** asked with passion
- **blood run cold:** blood become cold because it is so terrible
- **praised:** talked positively about

September 11th, 17--

We were completely free of the ice, and a passage to the south opened up. When the sailors saw this, they shouted with pleasure. This awoke Frankenstein, who asked why they were shouting.

'Because they will soon return to England,' I replied.

'Are you really returning?' he asked.

'I'm afraid so,' I answered. 'I cannot lead them into danger when they do not want to go.'

'Do what you want, Walton,' he said, 'but I will not go. My purpose is clear and I must follow my enemy.'

I called the ship's doctor. He said that Frankenstein had only a few hours left to live. Some time later he called me to him and said: 'Walton, I still wish for the death of my enemy. I created him, and I should kill him, but I have failed. Please promise me that you will kill him if you find him. The fact that he is still alive to do evil things when I am close to death, worries me.'

He died a few minutes later. I went out to get some fresh air. It was midnight and the ship was sailing towards England. Suddenly, I heard horrible sounds coming from my cabin. I ran downstairs and opened the door. There was the creature that Frankenstein had described, gigantic and ugly. He jumped towards the window when I entered. I have never seen anything more unpleasant than his face.

The monster looked at me and pointed towards Frankenstein.

'He is my victim, too,' he said. 'With his death it is all finished. Oh, Frankenstein, can I ask you to forgive me now, after I destroyed you by destroying all you loved? But he is cold. He cannot answer me.'

'You have carried your revenge too far,' I said, 'Frankenstein is now dead, thanks to you.'

'Do you think I enjoyed it?' asked the monster. 'When I returned to Switzerland, I pitied Frankenstein. I hated myself. But when I discovered that he dared to hope for happiness in things which I could never enjoy, I felt jealous. Then I wanted revenge for all my misery. This became my only passion. And now it is ended. There is my last victim!'

'Monster!' I cried. 'You do not feel pity. You are shouting only because the victim is dead and no longer in your power.'

'That is not true,' he interrupted. 'I once had dreams of being accepted by people for what I was like, not for my appearance. Crime has made me lower than the lowest, but even the worst criminals have family and friends. And here I am without a friend in the world. Alone. You seem to know my story. Why am I hated, and not Felix who drove me away, or the father who shot me when I saved his child? They are all good people, and only I am not. This is all so unfair and makes me very angry. It is true that I am terrible. I killed the young and innocent, those who never hurt me, and I made my creator's life a misery. There he lies, white and cold in death.

'You hate me, but your hate is not more than the hate I feel for myself. Do not worry, I will do no more wrong. My work is nearly complete. I will leave your ship on a piece of ice and find some wood to make a funeral fire. I will burn myself on the fire so that nobody else can find and recreate a creature like me. Only in death can I find rest and peace. Goodbye!'

And with this he jumped out of the cabin window onto the piece of ice which lay below and was soon carried away into the darkness.

After Reading

Personal Response

1 Did you enjoy reading the story? Why?/Why not?

2 What did you think of the ending of the story?

3 Did you feel sorry for the monster? Why?/Why not? Give your reasons and discuss with a partner.

4 Did you feel sorry for Victor Frankenstein? Did he deserve all the terrible things that happened to him?

5 Have you seen a film version of *Frankenstein*? Was the story different from the film or TV versions of *Frankenstein* you have seen? Make a list of the differences. Discuss with a partner. Which version did you prefer?

6 Does the story have a message for us? If so, what is it? Discuss in a pairs, then share with another pair.

7 The monster says: 'Please listen to me. I have suffered enough. I am your creature, and I will be gentle with you if you give me what you owe me… Make me happy and I'll be good.'
Do you think the monster was capable of keeping this promise to be good?

8 What do you think of the way Frankenstein behaved towards the monster? Could he have done anything differently? Write a few sentences and discuss with a partner.

After Reading

Comprehension

1 Tick (✓) true (T) or false (F).

	T	F
a) At the University of Ingolstadt, Frankenstein studied geography.	☐	☐
b) After Frankenstein created the monster he was filled with horror and disgust.	☐	☐
c) Elizabeth was Frankenstein's nurse when he was ill.	☐	☐
d) Frankenstein's father wrote to say his brother Ernest was dead.	☐	☐
e) Frankenstein went to the monster's shelter to hear his story.	☐	☐
f) The monster asked Frankenstein to make him a female companion.	☐	☐
g) Frankenstein did not agree to do this.	☐	☐
h) Frankenstein destroyed the female after he saw the monster looking at him.	☐	☐
i) The monster killed Henry Clerval when he and Frankenstein were in France.	☐	☐
j) Elizabeth was murdered by the monster just before the wedding.	☐	☐
k) Frankenstein left Geneva and followed the monster across Russia.	☐	☐
l) Frankenstein was in the North Pole when he was picked up by Walton.	☐	☐
m) After Frankenstein died the monster came onto the ship.	☐	☐
n) The monster was happy that Frankenstein was dead.	☐	☐

2 Frankenstein tells his story to Walton. Complete the sentences with the following words.

hate revenge letter science night monster deaths

a) I threw myself into the study of mathematics and ....

b) I wanted to produce a new species. I worked day and ....

c) But when I saw the ...., horror and disgust filled my heart.

d) Two years later I received a .... saying that my brother William was murdered.

e) I looked around our once-happy family. Everyone was destroyed because of the .... of William and Justine.

f) My desire for revenge and my .... of him filled my body and mind.

g) I beg you that you will kill him for me, to take ....

3 Ask and answer these questions with a friend.

a) Why did Frankenstein spend days and nights in tombs?

b) Why was the monster so tall?

c) What promise did Frankenstein make to the monster and then break?

4 What are these things and how were they important in the story? Make notes, then compare answers with a partner.

A

B

C

After Reading

Characters

1 Complete the sentences with the correct characters.

William	Justine Moritz	old blind man	Elizabeth
monster	Walton	Mr Krempe and Mr Waldman	

a) Frankenstein tells his story to .... as a warning.

b) Frankenstein's childhood was happy, especially after .... became part of his family.

c) .... were Frankenstein's professors at university.

d) Ernest and .... were the names of Frankenstein's brothers.

e) Frankenstein sometimes gave his creature names like '................' and 'devil'.

f) .... was the nanny who was executed for William's murder.

g) The .... lived in the cottage with Felix, Agatha and Safie.

2 Frankenstein says his idea was to: 'break through the knowledge of life and death and bring light into our dark world. I wanted to produce a new species that would bless me as its creator.' What does he mean? Tick (✓).

a) ☐ He wants to make a new race of people who will thank him.

b) ☐ He wants to make a new species for the good of all humans.

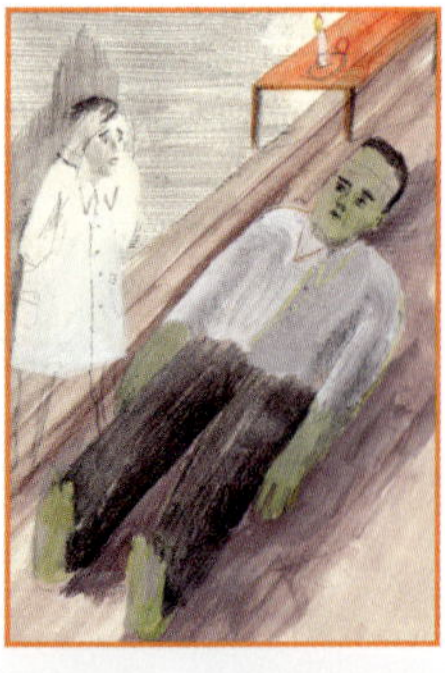

3 **The monster says: 'Misery made me into a monster. Make me happy and I'll be good.' What does he mean? Tick (✓).**

a) ☐ I behave badly because I am sad. If you are kind to me I'll be a nice person.

b) ☐ You created an evil monster, but you should have made a good one.

4 **Do you think the monster behaves badly because Victor is not kind to him? Why?/Why not? Discuss with a partner.**

5 **What do we learn about the monster in these parts of the story? Make notes.**

a) When he watches the people in the cottage.
b) When he saves the little girl who fell in the river and a man shoots him.
c) When Frankenstein destroys the female monster he is making.
d) When Frankenstein dies on Walton's ship.

6 **Read and say who is talking, Frankenstein or the monster.**

A But when I saw him, horror and disgust filled my heart.

☐ Frankenstein
☐ monster

B When night came I went out into the woods, wandering and howling. There was nobody who would feel pity for me or help me.

☐ Frankenstein ☐ monster

C Every day I feared he would do some new evil act.

☐ Frankenstein ☐ monster

D Do you dare to break your promise?

☐ Frankenstein ☐ monster

After Reading

Plot and Theme

1 **Put the events from the story in the correct order.**

1	2	3	4	5	6	7	8	9	10	11	12

a) But when he saw the monster, he was horrified and disgusted.

b) Justine Moritz was executed for William's murder.

c) Frankenstein grew up in Geneva and had a happy childhood.

d) He studied natural philosophy and chemistry at university.

e) The monster killed Elizabeth on her wedding night.

f) His brother William was murdered by the monster.

g) He discovered the cause of life and decided to make his own creation.

h) His friend Henry Clerval was found dead, murdered by the monster.

i) He followed the monster across Europe and Russia to the North Pole.

j) The monster vowed to kill himself and disappeared into the darkness.

k) Frankenstein died and Walton found the monster on his ship.

l) He went back to Geneva and made plans to marry Elizabeth.

2 In pairs, answer the questions.

a) Why does Frankenstein tell Walton his story?
b) What misfortune occurred in Frankenstein's life when he was seventeen?
c) How did Frankenstein react when he saw his creation?
d) Why did the monster enter the cottage when the blind man was alone?
e) How does the monster die?

3 Read the quotation and discuss the questions with a partner.

There was no-one like me. They talked of families, friends and children, but where were mine? My past life was completely empty. I had always been the same height and size, and I had never seen another being like me. What was I?'

a) How was the monster different from humans?
b) What things did the monster want? Find examples in the story.

4 Being ugly or different and how we treat people who are different is one of the themes of the story. Have you been in a situation where you felt different from other people around you? (Think of age, gender, race, etc.) How did you feel?

After Reading

Language

1 Complete this table with the words in the box.

graves mathematics regret philosophy funeral deathbed horror joy professor chemistry experiments cemetery despair lectures decay disgust anguish murderer science tombs

UNIVERSITY	EMOTIONS	DEATH
....	....	....
....	....	....
....	....	....
....	....	....
....	....	....
....	....	....

2 Complete the sentences with words from Exercise 1.

a) However, I decided not to go to his .... because Mr Krempe was an ugly, short, fat man.

b) Mr Waldman's first lecture began with a history of .... and recent developments.

c) I spent days and nights in .... watching the .... of human bodies.

d) I collected bones from the ...., the dissecting room and the slaughterhouse provided other parts I needed.

e) On my journey I was filled with mixed feelings: sadness at my little brother's death, and .... at seeing my father.

3 Complete the sentences with the correct form of the past perfect.

a) I .... (work) hard for nearly two years, but now the beauty of the dream .... (disappear).
b) I .... (begin) with good intentions. But I .... (destroy) everything.
c) When I awoke in the night, I saw the miserable monster I .... (create).
d) Next morning they told me, Justine .... (confess).
e) I told him about the very large man we .... (see) the day before.

4 Match the words to their definitions.

a) ☐ agony	1 bad luck
b) ☐ misery	2 reason for doing something
c) ☐ purpose	3 good behaviour
d) ☐ morals	4 not nice
e) ☐ misfortune	5 pain
f) ☐ unpleasant	6 great sadness

5 Change these sentences from direct to indirect speech.

a) 'You are all wrong,' I said. 'I know the murderer. Justine is innocent.'

....

b) 'Go away!' I shouted. 'I will not listen to you! We are enemies.'

....

c) 'I promise that I will live until I have taken revenge on this horrible monster.'

....

d) 'I swear,' he cried. 'If you agree you will never see me again. Now go and start your work.

....

After Reading

Exit Test

18 **1 Listen and tick (✓) the correct picture.**

a) 1 ☐  2 ☐ 

b) 1 ☐  2 ☐ 

c) 1 ☐  2 ☐ 

d) 1 ☐  2 ☐ 

P 2 Choose the correct answer 1, 2, 3 or 4.

a) Where was Walton sailing to when he saw Frankenstein?

1 ☐ Geneva | 2 ☐ Russia
3 ☐ The North Pole | 4 ☐ The Orkneys

b) When the monster observed the people in the cottage, he learned

1 ☐ how to play piano | 2 ☐ how to cook
3 ☐ how to read | 4 ☐ how to dance

c) To make a female companion for the monster, Frankenstein went to

1 ☐ the Orkneys | 2 ☐ Mont Blanc
3 ☐ Ingolstadt | 4 ☐ Russia

d) Who did the monster kill after Frankenstein's marriage?

1 ☐ William | 2 ☐ Elizabeth
3 ☐ Mr Waldman | 4 ☐ Walton

P 3 Read the sentences below. Complete the second sentence so it means the same as the first. Use no more than three words.

a) My main interest was the living body.
I was mainly .... the living body.

b) But when I saw the monster, horror and disgust filled my heart.
I was horrified .... when I saw the monster.

c) Every day I feared the monster would do some new evil act.
Every day I was worried the monster would do .... bad.

d) I will not create an evil companion for you.
I refuse .... evil companion for you.

After Reading

Project

WEB **Divide the class into three groups. Each group chooses a topic from below to research, preparing a presentation for the rest of the class, as a poster, on the Interactive White Board, or as a talk.**

GOTHICS AND ROMANTICS

Frankenstein is an example of a Gothic horror novel. Find out more about other Gothic novels and poems of the same time, *Dracula* for example. Find out also about the Romantic movement, which included the English poets Percy Shelley and Lord Byron. What did the Romantics believe? When did they write and what were their most famous works?

FILM AND TV VERSIONS

Find out which were the most important film and TV adaptations and when they were made. Did the film makers change or add to Mary Shelley's story? Find out as much information as you can, including which actors appeared in the films and which locations were used.

TRAVELS IN THE 18TH CENTURY

Research the places where Frankenstein travels in the story. Find information and pictures of places like the North Pole, Lake Geneva and Mont Blanc. Draw Frankenstein's route on a map. Find out about the importance of travel and the Grand Tour in the 18th century. Find out more about Mary Shelley's travels around Europe.